Jamaica's Find

Juanita Havill

Illustrated by Anne Sibley O'Brien

EGMONT

For Laurence-Aimée
J.H.

For my models, Brandy and Maygann
A.S.O'B.

First published ... emann Ltd
This edition published 2004 by Egmont Books Limited
239 Kensington High Street, London W8 6SA

Text © Juanita Havill 1986
Illustrations © Anne Sibley O'Brien 1986

A CIP catalogue record of this title is available from The British Library

ISBN 1 4052 0937 2
1 3 5 7 9 10 8 6 4 2

Printed in Italy

When Jamaica arrived at the park, there was no one there.
It was almost supper time, but she still had a few minutes to play.

She sat on a swing, and pushed off with her toes.
It was fun not to have to watch for the little ones
who always ran in front of the swings.

Then she climbed up the slide. There was a red woolly hat on the ladder step. Jamaica took it for a ride. She slid down so fast that she fell in the sand and lay flat on her back.

When she rolled over to get up, she saw a stuffed dog beside her. It was a cuddly grey dog, worn from hugging. All over it were faded food and grass stains. Its button nose must have fallen off. There was a round white spot in its place. Two black ears hung from its head.

Jamaica put the dog in her bicycle basket.

She took the hat to the park office and gave it to the young man at the counter.

The first thing her mother said when Jamaica came through the door was: "Where did that dog come from?"

"The park. I stopped to play on the way home," Jamaica said. "I found someone's red hat and took it to the Lost Property Office."

"But Jamaica, you should have returned the dog, too," said her mother. Then she said, "I'm glad you returned the hat."

"It didn't fit me," Jamaica said.

"Maybe the dog doesn't fit you either," her mother said.

"I like the dog," said Jamaica.

"Don't put that silly dog on the table!" Jamaica's brother said.

"You don't know where it came from. It isn't very clean, you know," her father said.

"Not in the kitchen, Jamaica," her mother said. Jamaica took the dog to her room. She could hear mother say, "It probably belongs to a girl just like Jamaica."

After supper Jamaica went to her room very quietly. She held the dog up and looked at it closely. Then she tossed it on a chair.

"Jamaica," her mother called from the kitchen.
"Have you forgotten? It's your turn to dry the dishes."
"Do I have to, Mother? I feel horrid," Jamaica answered.
Jamaica heard the pans rattle. Then she heard her mother's footsteps.

Her mother came in quietly, sat down by Jamaica,
and looked at the stuffed dog, which lay alone on the chair.
She didn't say anything. After a while she put her arms
around Jamaica and squeezed for a long time.

"Mother, I want to take the dog back to the park,"
Jamaica said.

"We'll go first thing in the morning." Her mother smiled.

Jamaica ran to the park office and plopped the stuffed dog on the counter.

"I found this by the slide," she told the young man.

"Hello! Aren't you the girl who gave me the hat last night?"

"Yes," said Jamaica, feeling hot around her ears.

"You certainly do find a lot of things. I'll put it on the Lost Property shelf."

Jamaica stood watching him.

"Is that all?" he asked. "You didn't find anything else, did you?"

"No. That's all." She stayed to watch him put the dog on a shelf behind him.

"I'm sure some little girl or boy will come in for it today, a nice little dog like that," the young man said.

Jamaica ran outside. She didn't feel like playing alone.
There was no one else in the park but her mother, who
sat on a bench. Then Jamaica saw a girl and her mother cross
the street to the park.

"Hi! I'm Jamaica. What's your name?" she said to the girl.

The girl let go of her mother's hand. "Kristin," she said.

"Do you want to climb the jungle gym with me, Kristin?" Jamaica said.

Kristin ran towards Jamaica. "Yes, but I have to find something first."

"What?" asked Jamaica. Kristin was bending under the slide.

"What did you lose?" said Jamaica.

"Edgar dog. I brought him with me yesterday and now I can't find him," Kristin answered.

"Was he kind of grey with black ears?" Jamaica couldn't keep from shouting. "Come along with me."

The young man in the park office looked over the counter
at the two girls.

"Now what have you found?" he asked Jamaica.

But this time Jamaica didn't drop anything onto the counter.
Instead, she smiled her biggest smile. "I found the girl who belongs
to that stuffed dog."

Jamaica was almost as happy as Kristin, who took Edgar
dog in her arms and gave him a big welcome-back hug.